An Improbable Adventure at Grandma's House

Sandra V. Konechny

AN IMPROBABLE ADVENTURE AT GRANDMA'S HOUSE
Copyright © 2024 by Sandra V. Konechny

All rights reserved. Neither this publication nor any part of this publication may be reproduced or transmitted in any form or by any means, electronic or mechanical, including photocopying, recording or any information storage and retrieval system, without permission in writing from the author.

Scripture quotations are taken from the Holy Bible, New Living Translation, copyright ©1996, 2004, 2015 by Tyndale House Foundation. Used by permission of Tyndale House Publishers, a Division of Tyndale House Ministries, Carol Stream, Illinois 60188. All rights reserved.

This is a work of fiction. Names, characters, places and incidents either are the product of the author's imagination or are used fictitiously, and any resemblance to actual persons, living or dead, businesses, companies, events, or locales is entirely coincidental.

ISBN: 978-1-4866-2435-5
eBook ISBN: 978-1-4866-2436-2

Word Alive Press
119 De Baets Street Winnipeg, MB R2J 3R9
www.wordalivepress.ca

Cataloguing in Publication information can be obtained from Library and Archives Canada.

Dedicated to
my grandchildren.

ACKNOWLEDGEMENTS

I want to express my appreciation for the people in my life who stimulate and inspire me. In this case, it's our grandchildren. Some of my greatest blessings call me Grandma.

My undying thanks go to my test readers, who, upon conclusion and without exception, ask for more of the same. That inspires me to keep writing more than anything else.

Thank you, Michael, for your full support when it came to the question of sharing this story with a wider audience than our immediate community.

Many thanks are extended to the editor and staff at Word Alive Press for their work in preparing this volume. You gave me good counsel.

Last, and certainly not least, my thanks and appreciation extend to the Lord Jesus Christ… the greatest storyteller of all. May all that I do bring glory to His name and character.

FOREWORD

The pictures hanging on the walls of my house are scenic. The one in the living room is large, depicting a forest of very tall trees with a gravel lane winding down the centre.

We are fortunate to have our married children living close by with their families. This means that the grandkids are occasionally brought over to hang out with their grandparents while their parents go about their business.

We play games together. One of them is to pretend we can walk into that forest picture and imagine the things, and what/whomevers, we discover when we go around the different bends, and what happens while we're there in that world that is beyond our own.

This story is born out of those imaginings…

CHAPTER ONE
Grandma's House

The small town of Dalmeny was home to Aidyn and Chase, the children of good, caring parents who worked at their own jobs most of the week in the large city of Saskatoon to the south. On days when school was closed, or when one of them became ill, they were often sent to their grandparents' house, on their dad's side, to pass the day being safely amused or get better.

Luckily, the house wasn't far. It was less than a ten-minute drive from their own home well into the country. In the summer, their daddy once made a Sunday afternoon outing of riding their bikes all the way to their grandparents' place. It was a bit tiring, but they made it and were rewarded for their efforts with cold drinks and an invitation to stay for dinner.

An Improbable Adventure at Grandma's House

Grandma's country home included Papa (who always seemed to be fixing things or cutting the grass on the riding lawnmower), a big white enthusiastic dog named Shep (short for Shepherd), three barn cats who didn't have real names but designations (mother cat, sister cat, and Killer), and two wethered pygmy goats named Merry and Pippin.

The small hobby farm also included a bit of forest that had walking paths cut through the trees. That bush contained a few climbing trees, a small, muddy pond that hatched tadpoles in spring, and a burn spot where Papa periodically burned dead wood, autumn leaves, and other rubbish. He was of a fastidious sort who couldn't abide messes of any kind around the yard.

There was also, within the little forest, a certain clearing that had arrows pinned to the trees, each pointing the way to such wonderful places as the North Pole, Narnia, Old Macdonald's Farm, Gotham City, Odyssey, and many other destinations. Wild fruit such as chokecherries, saskatoon berries, raspberries, plums, and even asparagus grew in the forest—though not every year, because they needed the right growing conditions to produce their crop.

One: Grandma's House

Grandma's house was rather typical of most grandmothers. It was a roomy place that featured a lot of old-fashioned items with some modern comforts mixed in. Aidyn and Chase's grandma was a collector of many things, including clocks. There was a clock in every room, even the bathrooms. She also collected jigsaw puzzles, dishes (mugs and assorted plates especially), and paintings to hang on the walls. These paintings were like windows that peeped into other worlds. They depicted ships at sea, houses that made you wonder who lived there, and scenes of nature that might remind you of times you went camping, canoed on a river, or went on some other lovely holiday.

Aidyn and Chase had visited their grandparents with regularity ever since they were born and never once noticed any oddities about the home. As far as they were concerned, it was just an ordinary place where the sofa and armchairs were comfy, the cookie jar was full, and the kitchen smelled of just-baked cinnamon buns or something else equally tantalizing.

An Improbable Adventure at Grandma's House

One: Grandma's House

But something soon happened to challenge that assumption, first to Chase and later to his sister and cousins as well. And that something made going to Grandma's house extra exciting.

CHAPTER TWO
Chase Disappears

It happened to Chase, one of the grandsons, the year he turned eight years old. It was a crazy, upside-down time when normal life stopped being normal. People suddenly became afraid of getting sick and stayed away from each other, assuming that everyone, including their friends and neighbours, were contagious with a new mystery disease. This fear caused the schools and businesses to close now and again.

But since the parents still had to work to pay the bills and keep food on the table, the children were sometimes brought over to spend the day at Grandma's house. Grandma said that she wasn't afraid of the mystery disease. She declared that most sicknesses could be gotten over by filling up on homemade chicken noodle soup or drinking

Two: Chase Disappears

hot lemonade. If not that, there were many other commonsense remedies that would help one get better.

On this particular day, Aidyn went outdoors to visit the goats and look around for the cats. Chase didn't feel like doing that. He complained of a headache and laid down on the sofa, hoping his pain would fade away. Grandma was nearby, puttering about in the kitchen. The little clattering noises Chase heard sounded like she was emptying the dishwasher.

As he lay on the sofa, his eyes naturally fell on the large painting hanging on the bit of wall located at the far side of the couch. It portrayed a forest of tall trees with a long, winding country road passing through it. It was easy to imagine that the road might lead to a lake or river somewhere because it wasn't wide and tarred like a highway.

Suddenly Chase saw movement in the painting. It appeared to be the backside of a man who had taken a step backward and then completely disappeared again as he took a step forward.

Surprised, Chase looked for the movement again but saw nothing more. He thought it must have been his imagination and was about to forget all about it

An Improbable Adventure at Grandma's House

when the backside of a man appeared again. He was wearing a camouflage cap and hoodie over baggy blue jeans with a red handkerchief partially hanging out of his rear pocket.

A second later, the man vanished again.

This time Chase got up. Standing on the other end of the sofa, he touched the picture along the right side of the frame, right around where he had seen the man. To his great surprise, his hand slid into the painting as neatly as if he'd walked into a neighbouring room.

Thoroughly curious, Chase dared to stick his head through the picture frame as well—and quickly found that he was looking into a very forested place, even though the rest of him was still in Grandma's living room. He noticed little sounds only heard in a forest, like the chirping of birds near and far, the buzzing of flies, and the ribbit of a frog in the distance.

Although Chase knew this was super strange, he wasn't afraid. What he saw and felt wasn't any scarier than walking around in the forest on Grandma's farm. And that wasn't scary at all.

Two: Chase Disappears

9

An Improbable Adventure at Grandma's House

Without another thought, Chase pulled himself up and climbed all the way into the painting.

At first he couldn't believe what he had just done. Was he still in his grandmother's living room? It certainly didn't seem like it. But it also didn't make sense that he was somewhere far away either. Yet that was how it appeared.

Another thing he noticed was that this place didn't look at all like the bush on Grandma's farm. Here, the trees were so tall that they looked like they touched the heavens.

A little nervous, Chase turned around, intending to climb down through the frame back into Grandma's living room. But all he saw was more forest. The road ahead was just as long and crooked as the one continuing in the opposite direction.

Now Chase felt afraid. Where was the picture frame that led back to Grandma's house? What if he was lost? What if he never saw his parents again? He tried very hard to look around for the opening to get back, but he couldn't find it anywhere. The best he could think to do was call out for his grandmother and hope she somehow heard him. Maybe if she figured out that he was calling from inside the

Two: Chase Disappears

painting, she would plunge her hand inside and show him where to get out.

Not knowing what else to do, and with tears forming in his eyes, Chase called in a loud voice: "Grandma! Grandma! Grandma, where are you?"

Of course, all that hollering got the attention of the strange person who had raised the boy's curiosity in the first place. Soon Chase heard tramping through the woods, and a moment later the man appeared standing in front of him.

"You've got a pretty big voice for a small boy," said the strange man, assessing the lad with crossed arms.

Chase hung his head shyly and didn't speak a word. He didn't yet know whether the stranger was friend or foe, but he was pretty sure it was the same man whose backside he had seen from Grandma's living room. After all, he wore a camouflage cap and hoodie over a pair of loose-fitting jeans. The man had a thick brown beard and blue eyes, eyes that looked at him kindly though his voice sounded gruff.

"Where are you from, son?" asked the stranger in a gentler tone. He squatted down to Chase's level.

An Improbable Adventure at Grandma's House

"I crawled in from my grandma's living room through a picture frame on the wall," said Chase hesitantly, knowing full well that the truth sounded ridiculous.

"Is that so?" The bearded man sounded thoughtful. "I heard there were such things that connected one world with another. But I haven't met anyone from the Beyond until now. What is your name, young feller?"

"Chase."

"Well, that's a good handle for a boy. I like it. You can call me Luccan. Make that Mr. Luccan, since I'm a grown man and you're still a tad."

"Can you show me how to get back to Grandma's house?" asked Chase softly and nervously.

"You're standing in front of the doorway."

Chase felt puzzled. "Then how come I can't see it?"

"Well now, it must be that the eyes you have don't quite work the same on this side of the picture." Luccan rubbed a hand over his beard and thought about it a few seconds longer. "Do you know what an autostereogram is?"

Chase shook his head.

Two: Chase Disappears

"It's a bit hard to describe, but I'll try. It's like taking a piece of colourful patterned paper and setting a recognizable shape on top of it with exactly the same pattern. At first glance, you can't see the shape at all. It just looks like an ordinary piece of flat patterned paper. But if you refocus your eyes in a special way, you'll see the image sitting clear as day on top. The way back through the picture is like that. The opening back to where you came from is shaped like a window, but it still looks just like the background of the forest. You have to refocus your eyes to see it as a separate three-dimensional object apart from the rest of the woods."

Chase looked again into the forest behind him. He squinted and then made his eyes as big as saucers. But no matter how hard he tried, he couldn't see the outline of the picture frame that connected the forest with Grandma's living room.

Luccan could see the boy was getting frustrated and fearful. "Don't give up now. It takes a bit of practice to convince your brain that your eyes can do more tricks than see the obvious."

To further help, he drew the outline of the opening with his arm, showing him where he should see it.

Chase continued to look at that space, tilting his head this way and that.

"Oh!" he finally said. "Now I see it. That's cool."

"You mean the air is colder by the opening?" asked Luccan, puzzled.

"No. I mean it's cool… I mean it's good."

"Well now, you just got here. Since you know the way back, how about you stay a few minutes longer and tell me about yourself?"

"I'm afraid my grandma will notice I'm gone." Chase sounded worried. "And she'll be scared that I'm lost or stolen or something. I'd better get back."

"I understand," said Luccan, "but I'm pretty sure you don't have to fret. I don't know much about these special pictures that act like bridges to the Beyond, but they seem to have the ability to fold time. What I mean is, when you go back to your grandma's living room, the time on the clock will only have moved ahead one second. Your grandma probably won't notice you were away at all. Aren't you curious about this place?"

"Yeah," admitted Chase. "That's why I crawled through the picture. But I didn't think the picture

Two: Chase Disappears

was more than a picture until I saw you in the corner appear and disappear. Am I still in Canada?"

Luccan frowned. "What's a Canada?"

"That's where I live. I can't believe you don't know about Canada."

"Do you know about Avery, mister smartie pants?"

"What's Avery?"

"Uh-huh, that's what I thought," said Luccan smugly. "Fact is, we each live in different worlds connected by the picture hanging in your grandmother's living room. I wonder how she came to have it. She probably doesn't realize that it has special, magical properties. Let me give you a piece of advice, Chase. When you go back, consider carefully how you might tell your grandmother, or anyone else, including your parents, about the adventure we're having. Don't be surprised if they just tell you that you have a great imagination but should stay grounded in the real world. But you know… and I know… that we met through very extraordinary circumstances, right?"

Chase nodded and then furrowed his eyes. "If you live in a different world than me, how come we speak the same language? Why do we understand each other's words?"

"Now that's a great question, Chase. And I don't know the answer. But as I think on it, I might have a good guess."

Chase waited for Luccan to offer his suggestion.

Luccan rubbed his beard again before speaking. "I think it's likely that your world and mine are made by the same Creator. Therefore, some things are the same from world to world."

The idea wasn't a big stretch for Chase. He already knew that his world had been created by God, and so was every planet and star in the universe. It was only common sense that if God made the earth, then He made all the other worlds, too.

"I expect you'll want to come back someday and explore this place a little more," said Luccan. "Do you see this here path?"

"Yes," answered Chase, noting the winding trail through the trees.

"It leads to the cabin where you can find me, or at least where you can wait until I get back from wherever I am." Luccan paused for a moment. "One more thing. I'll tie my red bandana to the branch

Two: Chase Disappears

closest to the portal in case you come and wander around and really do get lost. You'll know you're back where you should be when you see it."

"What's a portal?" asked Chase, confused again.

Luccan frowned. "How old are you?"

"Eight."

"Odd that the Great One would send a boy," mused Luccan to himself. "A portal is a gateway, or perhaps a window between two worlds. I showed you how to see it from this side. Apparently it's more obvious from the other side."

"Yes, it is," said Chase confidently. "I'd better go now. I don't want my grandma to worry. Bye, Mr. Luccan."

Luccan tousled the boy's hair. "See you again someday, if the Great One wills it."

As soon as Chase could see the outline of the frame, he poked his head through. The rest of him followed as he fell into the couch in Grandma's house with a loud tumble.

"Whatcha doing in there, Chase?" called his grandma from the kitchen. "You know you're not supposed to jump on the furniture."

"Sorry, Grandma."

Chase sat up straight and then turned to look at the picture from where he had just come. It no longer looked alive at all. He dared himself to touch it and found that it was just a canvas painting of a forest with a crooked road down the centre. How could that be? What was going on? He was sure that he had climbed into that picture and made a new friend named Mr. Luccan. How come it was just an ordinary picture again?

Needing answers, Chase lifted the painting a wee bit, only to have it come away from the wall. He had expected to see some kind of hole, or even a tunnel behind the picture, but there was only the plain old wall.

He then remembered Luccan's advice, about being careful about telling anyone of his experience because he wouldn't be believed. Now Chase understood exactly what Luccan had meant. He wasn't sure he believed it himself.

CHAPTER THREE
Aidyn Discovers a Mystery

Bored with entertaining the dog, Aidyn came back into Grandma's house through the front door. The blond, tall-for-her-age twelve-year-old kicked off her sneakers and began to walk down the hall towards the kitchen.

Hanging on the wall were two large paintings of tall ships at sea. Normally Aidyn wouldn't give these paintings a first thought, never mind a second, but for some reason she spotted a drop of water on the glass. It looked just like a raindrop, the kind that lands on a window when it first starts to rain.

Aidyn lifted her finger to wipe away the water. As soon as she took her hand away, a tiny stream of water trickled out of the painted ocean. Aidyn blinked, not believing her eyes.

But it was true. Water was seeping out of the painting and dripping onto the floor.

Even though it didn't make sense, Aidyn dashed to the kitchen, tore off a sheet of paper towelling, and ran back to the painting. Wadding up the paper, she pressed it onto the leak and waited. A minute later, she dared to lift the paper towel. Voila! The strange leak had stopped. The glass was as dry as it should be.

The painting next to it, however, was obscured in fog.

Frowning, Aidyn touched the glass, leaving behind her fingerprint. If she had wanted to, she could have printed her name on the wet, foggy glass with her finger. Instead she took the wadded-up paper towel in her hand and wiped away the mist. When she was done, it seemed to stay dry.

Mission accomplished, Aidyn came into the kitchen intending to throw the damp piece of paper towel into the trashcan. As she did so, however, her thoughts gave way to a hunch.

Next she went into the dining room where there hung another large painting, this one framed in three parts. They were landscapes of park-like forests with

Three: Aidyn Discovers A Mystery

a lake or river across the background. The centre one depicted a great tree in autumn with beautiful red leaves. Wind must have been blowing through it because the branches were swaying noticeably.

Curious, Aidyn reached into the picture and immediately felt a breeze cooling her hand. She withdrew it at once, and there sticking to her palm was a tiny red leaf. When she looked at the picture, however, the wind had stopped and the trees looked frozen in time again.

"Weird," said Aidyn to herself.

Her eyes fell on the mirror that hung on the end wall. Something about it, too, seemed unusual. It was still silvery and clear but appeared liquid-like. Without thinking of possible consequences, Aidyn reached up and touched the mirror. Sure enough, her finger broke through the surface as if it were pudding. When she removed it, the mirror went back to being completely smooth, although her finger retained some of the silver. Her fingertip sparkled.

"Grandma?" said Aidyn going back into the kitchen where her grandmother was getting ready to peel potatoes for supper at the kitchen sink.

"Yes, dear."

"Did you know the pictures in your house aren't normal?"

"No, I didn't," replied Grandma. "Why do you think so?"

"Because water was leaking out of the ships-at-sea pictures and I had to use paper towelling to wipe it up. And the wind was blowing the fall leaves around in the autumn picture. Even the mirror was all gooey, like melted silver."

Grandma raised her eyebrows as if to say, *That's sounds like a tall tale*.

"It's true," insisted Aidyn. She produced the damp lump of paper towelling but couldn't find the tiny red leaf. "See how my finger looks silvery where I poked it into the mirror?

She held her finger up to her grandmother's face.

Grandma peered at Aidyn's finger and then reached for her glasses. "Sorry, my dear, I can't see any fairy dust on your finger." She winked.

"I didn't say I had fairy dust on my finger," objected Aidyn. "It's a bit of silver from the mirror. You don't believe me, do you? I'm not lying, you know."

Three: Aidyn Discovers A Mystery

An Improbable Adventure at Grandma's House

"I believe you insofar as I know you to be a truthful grandchild. But I also know you like to tease your granny, and I'm thinking that's what you're doing now—pulling my leg for your amusement. That's all right. Grandma likes to have fun with you, too."

"Grandma, I'm serious."

"Well then, let's have a look." Grandma dried her hands before going to the next room.

"They've gone back to normal *now*," insisted Aidyn. "But they weren't normal a little while ago."

Grandma turned to look her granddaughter straight in the face. She saw Aidyn was in earnest and decided to take a different approach.

"I'm well aware that things aren't always as they seem," she began. "We live in a world that includes the supernatural. If you really believe the pictures and mirrors in the house have magical qualities, and it is indeed true, then beware. You may be in for some strange and wonderful adventures. But remember this: good and evil are real in every dimension. If you get into a Narnia-like adventure, there will be characters like Aslan and the White Witch somewhere about and you'll have to tell the

Three: Aidyn Discovers A Mystery

difference before you get into real trouble. Are you listening?"

"Yes, Grandma," said Aidyn blandly.

"Good. Now where has your little brother got to?"

CHAPTER FOUR
Aidyn and Chase Pay Luccan a Visit

A few days later, the children's parents called upon Grandma to watch Aidyn and Chase while they worked in the city. Their father was the stay-at-home parent now, but even he occasionally had to go on a road trip. On those days, Grandma's house was the most convenient solution.

Grandma didn't mind this arrangement at all. It filled her heart with joy to have her grandchildren around for a few hours.

Even while his daddy was driving to Grandma's house, Chase wondered whether the big forest picture in Grandma's house would come *alive* again so he could visit Luccan. He hadn't told anyone about his strange adventure. Sometimes he thought

Four: Aidyn and Chase Pay Luccan a Visit

it must have been something he dreamed up, not real. Other times he remembered Mr. Luccan so clearly that it had to be true. After all, he didn't know of any Mr. Luccan in Dalmeny or anywhere else in Canada.

Grandma met them at the door with hugs. She invited Aidyn to make a sweet yeast dough with which to bake cinnamon buns, one of their favourite snacks. Although Aidyn was only twelve, she could make yeast dough just about as well as any baker. Grandma was very proud of her. Baking from scratch seemed to have become a lost skill in so many homes.

Chase hung around the kitchen to watch the proceedings and sneak bits of dough and sugar whenever he thought he could get away with it.

But at one point he slipped into the living room to see if the big picture had come alive and opened. He was disappointed to find it flat.

Later, after the dough was made and set aside to rise, Aidyn slumped onto the couch to play for a while on the tablet she had brought with her. Having nothing else to do, Chase sat beside her to watch her play a game.

After a bit of time, he got bored and looked longingly at the forest painting. This time it looked different; the trees swayed slightly and he could feel the breeze on his face.

Without thinking, Chase stood on the sofa and climbed into the picture. Aidyn noticed the movement out of the corner of her eye and looked to the left just as his feet disappeared.

"Chase! What the…?"

Setting aside the tablet, Aidyn jumped up and looked through the picture as if it were an open window. She saw Chase land on the ground and scramble to get up.

"What's going on? How did you get in here?" demanded Aidyn with a mixture of amazement and fear.

"I don't know." Chase rubbed the dust off his pants. "It happened once before by accident. I've been watching all day to see if the picture came alive again, because then you could come in here, too. Last time I met a man, and his name was Mr. Luccan. He said if I came again I could come to his cabin to visit."

Four: Aidyn and Chase Pay Luccan a Visit

"I'm scared, Chase," said Aidyn nervously. "You'd better get back in here before something awful happens. What if the magic stops while you're away and then you can't get back?"

"Mr. Luccan said that time would fold and it would be like we were never away at all," said Chase. "Come with me and see for yourself."

"If you're not going to come back, I guess I have no choice but to go with you. No way are you allowed to wander around in a strange place by yourself."

With that, Aidyn climbed the rest of the way into the painting. As soon as she was through, she looked behind her and nearly fainted.

"Grandma's house is gone!" she shrieked in a panicked voice.

"No, it isn't," said Chase, unflapped. "Calm down. See the red hanky tied to the branch?"

Aidyn nodded.

"It marks the spot that connects with Grandma's living room," he added. "We'll come here after we visit with Mr. Luccan and get back home to our own world, easy peasy. You'll see."

An Improbable Adventure at Grandma's House

30

Four: Aidyn and Chase Pay Luccan a Visit

"You had better be right, little brother." Aidyn sounded doubtful. "Because I want to be back at Grandma's house when Mom and Dad come for us."

Chase remembered where to look for the path off the main road, just as Luccan had shown him. They followed it now, feeling rather excited and a little afraid, not knowing whether the forest was safe or not.

It wasn't long, however, before the path opened into a spacious clearing. On the edge stood a small log cabin with a veranda on which was stationed a willow rocking chair. The door was slightly open and smoke escaped through the chimney.

"Mr. Luccan. Mr. Luccan!" called Chase loudly as he approached the cabin.

Soon a bearded man filled the doorway. He squinted, trying to figure out who his visitors were. He smiled broadly upon recognizing Chase.

"So you've come again! I wasn't sure you would," said Luccan with a chuckle. "You, I remember. Your name is Chase, right?"

Chase nodded.

"But who have you brought with you?"

"This is my sister, Aidyn," replied Chase. "She saw me go into the picture and wouldn't let me be here by myself. So she came along. I wanted to see you before going back to Grandma's living room."

"Hmmm. Good for you, Aidyn. Looking after your little brother is right responsible of you. You're looking a little green, though. Aren't you feeling well?"

"I'm kinda scared," admitted Aidyn. "Where is this place?"

"You are in the land of Avery."

"Is it safe here? Are there dangers?"

Luccan didn't answer her question immediately. He scanned the edges of the clearing for a moment and then looked directly at Aidyn. "Let's just say you're safe with me."

"Can we see inside your cabin?" asked Chase, full of curiosity.

"Well, sure. I was just about to fix myself a hot refreshing drink. I'll make enough for all of us."

Luccan opened the door wide and led them inside. They stepped into the one-room cabin that displayed a single bed in one corner and an armchair in the one opposite. A small table and two chairs stood at the other end of the cabin along with a few cupboards that resembled a kitchen.

Four: Aidyn and Chase Pay Luccan a Visit

A double-sided stone fireplace warmed the cabin from the middle of the room. Hanging over the small fire was a steaming kettle that was spitting a few drops of liquid.

"Aahh, our tea is ready," said Luccan, pleased.

He quickly withdrew three cups from a cupboard, along with a plate on which he placed a few pieces of something that looked almost like cookies. He set these on the table and indicated that Chase and Aidyn should sit in the chairs while he brought in a log on which to seat himself.

"This tea is delicious," said Aidyn. "It tastes like fruit and flowers."

Luccan smiled. "I'm glad you like it. And what about you, young man? Are you enjoying the snack? I made them just this morning."

"Not bad," replied Chase. "I've never had this before, but it tastes good."

"I suspect food might be different where you're from."

Just then, a cat pushed the door open and began to meow loudly. Luccan meowed back and they meowed back and forth for a couple of minutes.

Luccan seemed to have the last word, however. The cat became quiet, jumped onto the armchair, and made herself comfortable.

Aidyn looked at Luccan disbelievingly. "If I didn't know better, I'd say you were talking cat language… with a cat," she said doubtfully.

"Of course I did! How else am I to learn how her day went? Not only do I speak cat, but I can converse in a few other animal languages as well."

"Are you serious?" piped up Chase. "We can't do that in our world."

Luccan looked amazed. "You don't talk to animals in your world?"

"Well, we do, like giving commands in our language, but they don't talk back," answered Chase.

"But how do you exchange information or express feelings and needs if you don't communicate on their level?"

"We manage by observing and reading behaviour," declared Aidyn. "What other animal languages do you know?"

Luccan stroked his beard. "I know cat, dog, rabbit, squirrel, raccoon, deer,

Four: Aidyn and Chase Pay Luccan a Visit

goat, cow, crow, chicken, horse, and a bit of bear. Not that I'm bragging, mind you."

"What about other people? Do you have neighbours?" asked Aidyn.

"Not exactly. I'm a forester in the service of the Great One. This is my district to look after."

"Don't you get lonely?"

Luccan answered as if the question was silly. "The Great One keeps company with me. Why should I be lonely?"

"Chase, we ought to be heading back. Grandma will worry when she can't find us." Aidyn clearly meant that although visiting with Mr. Luccan was interesting, it was time to leave.

"Your sister is right," said Luccan. "I have duties to attend to and can't take the time to walk you back to the portal. I'll call on Prince to escort you."

Luccan went to the door and barked in short, clipped woofs. Pretty soon a handsome German Shepherd came bounding across the clearing. Luccan held the door open so he could come inside. The dog greeted Luccan with a couple of short woofs and a long howl. Luccan answered in woofs of different lengths and timbres. It was an astonishing and weird conversation for Aidyn and Chase to listen to.

When they had finished, Luccan turned to the children. "Prince assures me that the woods in our district are quiet today. By that, I mean that there are no enemy forces attempting to do mischief or worse. You could probably get to your portal without interference. But Prince has agreed to take you back to the main road to ensure your safety." He ushered Chase and Aidyn outdoors. "If the Great One wills it, we'll see you next time."

The kids thanked Mr. Luccan for their refreshments and waved goodbye. Prince led them back along the same path on which they had come, with his ears perked for the smallest unnatural sounds whilst sniffing the air.

Soon they were back at the spot where the red hanky hung on a tree branch.

"I still don't see how we get back into Grandma's house," grumbled Aidyn anxiously.

"Just give me a minute. I'll figure it out." Chase stared hard in front of him. After a moment, he said, "Got it! Come with me."

Four: Aidyn and Chase Pay Luccan a Visit

Chase grabbed Aidyn's hand and made a motion like poking his head through a window. Sure enough, beneath them they saw Grandma's plaid sofa. Carefully they lifted their legs and stepped all the way inside.

Aidyn sighed with relief as she sat down. She saw that her tablet was exactly where she'd set it aside.

"Did that just happen or was it a dream?" she said to Chase, who was staring intently at the painting out of which they'd just come.

"It really happened, but look. The magic is over. The picture is flat again. We can't go inside now."

"I wonder how it works. I mean, is it like a regular set time or just random chance?"

"I don't know," said Chase. "Luccan thinks it's when the Great One wants it to happen… whoever He is."

CHAPTER FIVE
Aidyn and Chase Discuss Grandma's House

"Did you have fun today?" asked Aidyn and Chase's mother after she had picked up her children and was on the drive home.

"Yup!" said both kids at the same time.

"What did you do?"

"I made cinnamon buns with Grandma. She let me make the dough by myself from scratch," answered Aidyn.

Chase added, "She said we could help ourselves to eating peas and strawberries right out of the garden whenever we wanted."

"We tried to teach Shep to fetch with a stick." Aidyn let out a giggle. "He picks up the stick, all

Five: Aidyn and Chase Discuss Grandma's House

right, but he won't give it back. He changes the game from fetch to tag. And he won't let us catch him!"

"Sounds like you had fun," commented their mother. "Anything else?"

"Yeah," admitted Chase. "We walked the trail in the forest."

Aidyn and Chase exchanged glances regarding that last bit. Strictly speaking, it was true. But they knew very well that their mother would assume they meant the trails through the woods on their grandparents' acreage.

Still, it didn't seem right to talk about the magical moments they had experienced in Grandma's living room. So they let it slide and their mom seemed none the wiser.

Because he was younger, Chase had to go to bed a half-hour earlier than Aidyn. However, as soon as their mother kissed Chase goodnight and left his room, Aidyn crept quietly from her bedroom and opened his door a crack.

"Chase, can I come in?" whispered Aidyn. "I want to talk."

An Improbable Adventure at Grandma's House

"Okay," said Chase.

Aidyn quietly closed the door behind her and parked herself at the end of his bed. "I can't stop thinking about what happened today," she began in a soft voice. "It's so weird that the pictures in Grandma's house are enchanted. It's kind of exciting, but also a little scary."

"I only know that the picture by the sofa is magical," said Chase. "I was lying down on the couch because I had a headache. Then I saw the bum of somebody appear and disappear in the big painting on the wall. I got up to see what was going on and that's when I discovered it was like a door to another place. How do you know the rest of the pictures are special, too?"

"I came back into the house after playing with the cats and stuff and noticed the ocean paintings in the hallway were foggy and leaking water. That's never happened before. On a hunch, I went to the dining room and saw that the autumn picture was alive, with wind blowing the leaves off the trees. Even stranger was the big mirror! I could stick my finger into it as if it were pudding. It came out shiny and silvery. But then they all went back to normal."

Five: Aidyn and Chase Discuss Grandma's House

An Improbable Adventure at Grandma's House

Chase leaned on his elbow. "Does Grandma know her house is sort of peculiar?"

"I actually pointed it out to her after I wiped up the wet from the hallway and stuck my finger into the mirror," said Aidyn, shifting from sitting down to lying on her stomach. "She didn't believe me at first and said I was only pulling her leg. But when I insisted that I was telling the truth, she admitted that the world could be a strange place sometimes. She also said that if the pictures really did have mysterious powers, and we ended up having extraordinary experiences, we have to be careful. Those places have forces of good and evil which can be confusing and dangerous."

They heard scratching on the door and Aidyn got up to let in their big black dog, Sydney. Immediately the dog jumped on the bed and curled himself up beside Chase. Aidyn propped up her feet on Sydney's back. Now the bed was crowded. Chase squirmed and fidgeted, trying to get comfortable.

"I think Mr. Luccan is good," he said defensively, returning to their conversation.

"I think so, too. But remember when I asked him if it was safe in his area? He said that we were

Five: Aidyn and Chase Discuss Grandma's House

protected when we were with him. To me, that means it's not a safe place to explore on our own."

"But I want to go back," insisted Chase. "I'm not scared to climb into the picture when it comes alive."

"That's another thing," said Aidyn. "The picture isn't alive all the time. We don't know if it happens on a schedule or by chance. We're not at Grandma's house every day either, so how do we know how often the pictures open up to other places?"

Chase frowned. "Mr. Luccan says that it will happen when the Great One wants it to. Who do you think that is?"

"I've been thinking about that. My guess is that in our world, we call him God."

"Oh… I see." It was like a lightbulb went off in Chase's head. "If God is Mr. Luccan's friend, then we *are* safe with him. We know that God loves us and cares for us, so that means…"

Unexpectedly, the door opened and their mother poked her head inside. "I thought I was hearing noises. What's going on in here? Why aren't you in your own room getting ready for bed, Aidyn?" she asked with increasing crossness.

"I just wanted to tell Chase something before I forgot," explained Aidyn.

"Well, make it quick! It's your bedtime now, too."

Their mother left the door open as she walked away.

"What I mean is, we don't know who or what to be careful of where Mr. Luccan lives," said Aidyn softly when she was sure Mom was out of earshot.

Chase yawned. "That's something we can ask Mr. Luccan next time we see him."

"I want to see him again too," agreed Aidyn. "I'm just saying we have to be careful. We might be playing with fire."

"I think the Great One—God—will look after us."

"I suppose you're right. It makes me wonder why, though."

"What do you mean?"

"I wonder why God—the Great One—would cause us kids to go into another world," Aidyn said. "There must be a reason… not just for having fun."

"Mr. Luccan wonders about that, too," said Chase, remembering a comment Luccan had once made.

"Anyway, it's no excuse to be careless. I want you to promise me something."

Five: Aidyn and Chase Discuss Grandma's House

"What?" asked Chase sleepily.

"Promise me you'll never go to Mr. Luccan's world by yourself, that we will always go together. Okay?"

"Okay."

"Pinky swear!"

The brother and sister hooked little fingers to seal their promise.

CHAPTER SIX

The Cousins Meet a Clown

A couple of weeks later, another set of grandkids came to spend the day with Grandma. The three of them, two boys and one girl, were city dwellers. Their daddy was a fine carpenter, and on this day he intended to build something for their mother in Grandpa's shop.

The eldest was eight-year-old Kipton, a thoughtful, dark-haired boy who liked to read and spend hours hovered over a table full of tiny toy bricks. His imagination for building spacecraft was unlimited.

His blond six-year-old sister Oakley loved the colours pink and purple, as well as all sparkly things. She loved to be part of anything and everything Grandma had on the go in the kitchen.

Six: The Cousins Meet a Clown

Chubby little brother Bodhi was three and very talkative. Talking too much made him slow to finish his dinners, and he annoyed his parents and siblings when they tried to concentrate. But he was so adorable that no one could be irritated with him for long. Despite his motormouth, he was everyone's favourite kiddo.

These grandkids knew their cousins lived nearby and pleaded with Grandma to see them. "Can we invite Chase and Aidyn to come and play with us?"

"That's a good idea," agreed Grandma. "We'll give them a call."

Having more of her grandchildren around would actually make the day easier for her. They played with each other so happily that she wouldn't need to entertain them much at all.

Soon Aidyn and Chase were brought over and Grandma's living room was filled with the sounds of laughing, noisy children. The boys brought up the tub of building blocks their fathers had played with when they were boys.

Meanwhile, Aidyn tried to braid Oakley's unruly hair. She kept looking up at the painting at the end of the sofa, though, and eventually Oakley noticed.

An Improbable Adventure at Grandma's House

"Why do you keep looking at that picture, Aidyn? It's not new."

"Oh, just because," replied Aidyn evasively.

These comments caused Chase to look up from his building project. He gasped and pointed to the painting. "It's alive again, Aidyn!"

Every kid's eyes turned to look. Chase immediately jumped up on the sofa and began to climb in. The rest began to talk at the same time.

"Hey… what are you doing?" called Kipton as he jumped up on the sofa after him.

Oakley's eyes opened wide. "What's happening?"

"Wait, Chase!" objected Aidyn. "I don't think we should go today."

Bodhi climbed up on the sofa and stood beside Kipton, not wanting to be left out of the commotion.

"Let's all go and see Mr. Luccan," said Chase, his voice coming from the other side of the frame.

"How did you do that?" asked a puzzled Kipton. What he saw defied all logic.

"I don't know. It's some kind of magic that happens once in a while," answered Chase. "I've done it before. It's okay. We get back home before Grandma evens knows we're gone."

48

Six: The Cousins Meet a Clown

Aidyn sounded doubtful. "I'm not sure about this."

Nevertheless, after Kipton climbed into the picture she helped Oakley over the frame, lifted Bodhi in, and then brought up the rear herself.

Chase wanted to lead them all along the path that led to Luccan's cabin, but movement far up the crooked road caught his eye. From far away it looked like a butterfly flitting its way towards them. As it drew closer, the colourful thing took on arms and legs.

"Hey, it's a clown!" said Kipton, astonished but smiling.

The children watched in mesmerized wonder until the clown, skipping and somersaulting, landed on his feet in front of them. He bowed deeply and with fanfare.

"What have we here?" The clown gazed into their eyes one by one. "I don't recall seeing any of you before."

"We're new here," piped up Oakley with eyes as wide as saucers. "Can you do tricks?"

"Of course I can. What were you thinking of?" replied the clown. His smile was mostly painted, but it stretched across his entire face.

An Improbable Adventure at Grandma's House

Six: The Cousins Meet a Clown

"Can you pull a rabbit out of a hat?" wondered Chase.

"Watch this!" Suddenly a tall black hat appeared in the clown's hands. He showed the children that it was empty and even stuck his finger through a hole on top. Then he waved his hand over it and said, "Abracadabra!"

The next thing they knew, he pulled a brown bunny out of his hat by the ears and presented it to Oakley.

"Can you do card tricks?" asked Kipton, intrigued.

Immediately the clown produced a deck of cards, seemingly out of thin air, and began shuffling them with fancy cuts and movements.

He focused on Kipton. "Pick a card… any card… from anywhere in the deck."

Kipton drew a card and, after memorizing it, returned it to the clown.

After some more fancy shuffling, he showed Kipton a card. "Is this the card you drew?"

Kipton smiled. "It's the right number, but not the right suit."

"You have a good memory," said the clown approvingly. "I believe this is the right one." He pulled a card from behind his ears and showed it to Kipton.

"Hey! That *is* the right one."

The clown did a trick for each of the children, including juggling some balls for little Bodhi. And as he performed, he asked questions of a personal nature.

"Where do you live?"

"At home," said Chase. "In Canada."

"Have you ever been here before?"

"Yes," said some of the cousins. "No," said others.

"How did you get here?"

"Through Grandma's picture," answered Kipton, his eyes getting bigger and bigger with astonishment.

"But that's only when it comes alive," added Chase.

The clown turned to Aidyn. "How old are you?"

"Twelve and a half," she replied absentmindedly, focusing on the clown's juggling, which was now up to eight balls.

"I'm on my way to do a show. Would you like to come along with me?"

Six: The Cousins Meet a Clown

"Yes!" said Oakley right away.

"No!" Aidyn was firm. "We have to go back to Grandma's living room."

"But first we have to visit with Mr. Luccan," insisted Chase.

The clown became suddenly horrified. "Mr. Luccan! You know this man?"

Aidyn and Chase looked at each other, uncertain about how to respond. "He's our new friend," said Chase slowly.

The clown leaned towards them and whispered in a conspiratorial fashion, "Beware of Mr. Luccan. He can be dangerous to children. I would avoid him at all costs."

On that disturbing note, he quickly left them. He continued to skip and somersault down the road as he had before.

"I think that's enough adventure for one day," said Aidyn. "Let's get back to Grandma's living room. Now."

But Chase wouldn't budge. "I'm not going back until I've seen Mr. Luccan."

"The clown said he could be dangerous," protested Aidyn. "We don't know him very well, after all."

Suddenly Prince, the German Shepherd, showed up, wagging his tail happily. He licked Bodhi's face and nuzzled the other children with his nose.

"Prince, is Mr. Luccan a good guy?" asked Chase, getting directly to the point.

Prince barked a single, sharp woof.

"That sounded like a yes to me," said Chase. "Come on. Let's go."

CHAPTER SEVEN

Luccan Explains the Trickster

The dog led the children down the forest path towards Luccan's cabin, sniffing left and right as he loped along. When they reached the clearing, Prince barked furiously. The sound brought Luccan to the door to see what the hullabaloo was all about. While he promptly recognized Aidyn and Chase, he was curious about the other three children.

"These are our cousins," explained Chase. "We're all at Grandma's house today. When the picture came alive, we brought them along to see you."

"We also saw a clown," Oakley continued in a rush. "He did lots of tricks for us."

"A clown, you say." Luccan seemed suddenly suspicious. "What did he look like? What did he do? What did he say?"

The children began to talk at once, describing his amazing tricks and clownish stunts. Luccan had to listen carefully to sort out all the details.

When they had finally finished talking, Luccan gave them a very serious expression. "My dear children, I believe you have met the Trickster. I can't say I'm surprised. It was bound to happen sometime, but it's not good."

"Why isn't it good?" piped up Oakley.

"Because *he's* not good."

Luccan went inside his cabin and soon returned with a blanket which he spread on the ground. When he invited the children to sit down on it, Bodhi made himself comfortable on Aidyn's lap. Luccan sat, too, and continued with his explanation.

"The Trickster is the land of Avery's nemesis…"

"I don't know what a nemesis is," said Chase.

"Me neither," added Kipton and Oakley together.

Luccan nodded. "It means he is an adversary."

"I don't know what that is either," Chase shook his head.

Seven: Luccan Explains the Trickster

"Well, how about enemy?" asked Luccan.

All the children nodded, including Bodhi, though it wasn't clear the little boy truly understood. He was just happy to be included.

"All right, the Trickster is the archenemy of the Great One," continued Luccan. "It wasn't always that way, but long ago, when he was second in command of Avery, he got jealous of the Great One. He wanted to be the king and in charge of everything. In short order, he got fired for his mutiny. Instead of going away, though, he hangs around to make trouble for everyone in our country, especially those who remain loyal to the Great One."

"How does he make trouble?" asked Kipton, wanting to understand more fully.

"If the Great One says 'Come up,' the Trickster says 'Go down.' If the Great One says 'White,' the Trickster says 'Black.' If the Great One says 'Go,' the Trickster says 'Stay.' If the Great One says 'Obey,' the Trickster says 'Rebel.' And on and on like that."

Chase frowned in a way that showed he was thinking hard. "Why does he wear a clown costume?"

An Improbable Adventure at Grandma's House

58

Seven: Luccan Explains the Trickster

"Good question, boy. He has many costumes that he uses to beguile his targets. In fact, it's not only costumes. He's a shapeshifter."

"What's that?" asked Aidyn, becoming concerned. As the oldest, she felt responsible for Chase and her cousins. She didn't like it at all that they might be in danger from a dishonest clown.

"It means he takes on any shape he thinks will successfully lure one away from the Great One. If he means to seduce you, he may present himself as a clown, or a sweet old grandpa, or perhaps a big cuddly sheepdog. Something that seems friendly and innocent. If he thinks it will require force, he may take on the shape of a terrible monster, an ugly witch, or perhaps a dangerous animal or snake. On the other hand, he may present himself as a resourceful one who can help someone get what they want, such as riches, or fame, or beauty… whatever one's heart's great desire might be."

Oakley folded her arms across her chest. "The clown we met didn't seem like he meant to do us any harm."

Luccan looked at Oakley with steady eyes. After a few seconds, he placed a finger under her chin and tipped it up so she could meet his gaze.

"Dear child," he began gently. "I have this very uneasy feeling that the Trickster has already won you over with his shenanigans. You must resist his charms or it will soon go badly for you."

"This is all very confusing," Aidyn said. "The clown really did seem harmless and didn't do anything worse than make us laugh and amaze us with his tricks. He warned us that *you* were dangerous to children and should be avoided. Since we don't know you very well, I'm not sure who to believe."

Luccan's face fell. He shook his head sadly before speaking. "The Trickster hates me because I serve the Great One. As much as he tries, he cannot budge my loyalty to Him. My job as forester is to keep the Trickster from polluting this area of the royal forests so the animals who live in these parts have everything they need to live. From all the many times I've tangled with the Trickster, I know him to be a liar, thief, imposter, cheat, and all-around scoundrel. It makes my blood boil to hear of the ways he's attempting to deceive you when you're so new to

Seven: Luccan Explains the Trickster

Avery. And speaking of which, it's still a mystery to me why the Great One allows you to come here. I cannot figure out the purpose in it."

"Does it have to have a purpose?" asked Chase innocently. "Maybe it's just for fun."

"I know for sure that the Great One doesn't mind his subjects enjoying life's pleasures, but I doubt it's that simple for you to come from another world into this one without a special reason." Luccan's sadness and anger had been replaced with real curiosity.

Prince had been lying next to Luccan, listening to the entire discussion without so much as a whimper. Suddenly he got up and began to growl softly while sniffing the air.

"He smells the Trickster nearby, or perhaps one of his followers," explained Luccan. "Good dog, Prince."

"That's amazing!" Kipton said. "There's no one else here but us, and still your dog can smell someone far away?"

"Prince has an amazing nose," agreed Luccan. "It's a special gift from the Great One so he can

61

serve Him well. But he doesn't need it to detect the Trickster. Anyone can smell him a mile away if they recognize his unique stink. It's far worse than any skunk I know. You must have caught a whiff of it when he was performing his tricks for you."

"Actually, I did notice he smelled kind of bad," granted Aidyn. "It reminded me of how stinky I get from playing hard and sweating at my hockey games. He smelled like stale sweat, like he should have a shower."

"Now that you mention it, I smelled it too," said Chase. "But I thought it was because of all his skipping and somersaulting."

"That settles it for me," declared Luccan. "Now I'm certain the clown you met was the Trickster. Even if he took a thousand showers, he would still smell bad, because he's rotten to the core. Water and soap can't wash that away. I'll take you back to the portal myself to make sure he doesn't try to fascinate you any further."

Realizing that the time had come to return to Grandma's living room, the children followed Prince as the dog led them away, trotting briskly like the

Seven: Luccan Explains the Trickster

good soldier he was. Luccan came last, giving little Bodhi a piggyback.

When they reached the portal, near the hanging red bandana, Luccan said, "Besides Chase, does anyone else know how to see the window to your world?"

They all shook their heads.

"Then you need to learn." Luccan went on to explain again what an autostereogram was. It took several tries, but eventually Aidyn and Kipton caught on. He patiently worked with Oakley until she got the hang of it, too.

Bodhi didn't get it at all, but they agreed he would always be with someone who could carry him over.

When Luccan was satisfied that the bigger children had learned the key to the portal, he bade them goodbye and sent them through the picture frame.

They landed in a heap on the couch.

"Ouch! Get off me, Kipton!" griped Oakley.

"I will as soon as Chase gets off me…"

It took a few seconds to sort themselves out. Then Grandma called from the kitchen.

"Lunchtime! Everyone wash their hands and come to the table."

The children looked at each other as if they weren't sure what to tell her of their adventures. Aidyn held a finger in front of her lips, a code for them not to say anything at all—at least not for the moment.

CHAPTER EIGHT
Oakley's Temptation

After lunch, Grandma shooed the children outdoors to play and get some fresh air. They decided to visit the strawberry patch at the far end of the garden to pick and eat strawberries for their dessert.

Although the berries were awesomely delicious, this activity lasted only about ten minutes. After that, Kipton and Chase took the bikes out for a spin. Bodhi begged Aidyn to take him to see the goats, Merry and Pippin. Oakley would have gone with them but found that she needed to use the bathroom; she came back into the house, meaning to catch up with Aidyn.

When Oakley passed the living room, she was reminded of the strange yet wonderful adventure they'd had that morning. She couldn't help but

An Improbable Adventure at Grandma's House

wonder whether the picture had come alive again. So instead of going back outside, she veered into the living room and went straight to the big painting.

She reached up to touch the painting and found that her hand went straight through! Delighted, she got up onto the sofa and climbed inside. She then looked down the curvy country road, half-expecting to see the clown come bounding towards her just as he had that morning. When there was no action in that direction, she turned around and started from fright. Very close behind her was the clown, sitting on a chair and grinning through large painted lips that smiled from ear to ear.

"You scared me!" said Oakley, feeling extra pink from head to toe.

"I didn't mean to," said the clown pleasantly. "I only hoped you would come back, and here you are. Where are the others?"

"They're playing outside. Do you want me to go and get them?"

"That won't be necessary, pretty girl. How about you and I get acquainted? Tell me about yourself. What are your favourite things? You can sit on my lap if you like."

Eight: Oakley's Temptation

By this time, Oakley had overcome the fear of surprise and felt quite comfortable with the clown. She climbed onto his lap as easily as if he had been Santa Claus in the mall. She noticed that he smelled funny, like he needed a bath, but quickly decided that it wasn't unusual. Everyone smelled dirty sometimes; that's why everyone's house had a bathtub.

Oakley batted her eyelashes. "Can you guess my favourite candy?"

"Oh, aren't you the coy one," said the clown in his most charming tone. "I bet you like them all."

"Yes, I do. But my favourtist is a big twisty, rainbow lollipop."

"I knew it!" The clown set Oakley on the ground so he could stand up. The first thing he did was fold the chair several times until it was a small cube. He placed it in his pocket.

"How did you do that?" asked Oakley, amazed.

"I'm a clown who performs magic, and I'm very good at it."

The clown then reached into the pocket on the other side of his costume and felt around. It seemed like the pocket went all the way down his pantleg to

An Improbable Adventure at Grandma's House

his shoes! Oakley found this very funny and laughed in delight.

At last the clown seemed to find what he was after. Presto! He pulled out a giant rainbow lollipop and handed it to Oakley with a flourish.

Oakley's eyes went as wide as they could possibly get. "That's the biggest lollipop I've ever seen!"

Again the clown smiled broadly and took a bow. "Tell me what else you would like to have. My pockets are full of tasty and lovely things."

"Well, in that case, how about some sparkly nail polish?"

The clown showed Oakley his closed fist and then opened it. There lay a little bottle of bright pink, and silver sparkly nail polish.

Oakley's eyes nearly fell out of her head. "How did you do that?"

The clown smiled his most charming smile. "A professional clown and magician doesn't divulge the secrets of his trade. I'm sure there must be other things on your wish list. Ask me for anything you would like to have, Oakley."

"Anything? Seriously?"

Eight: Oakley's Temptation

"Your wish is my command."

"I love beautiful dresses—the kind that princesses wear," said Oakley after another lick of her lollipop.

This time the clown reached inside his sleeve and pulled out a scarf, and then another and another and another until it seemed the chain of scarves was endless. Oakley laughed and laughed, clapping her hands.

"I seem to have forgotten where I've put the princess dresses," said the clown sheepishly. "I'll have to try something else."

He reached behind his back and pulled out a wand with a star on the end that sparkled like diamonds.

"This will do." He looked directly into Oakley's eyes. "Abracadabra!"

With a flourish, he touched her shoulder—and instantly Oakley's jeans and T-shirt were transformed into a beautiful pink and white ballgown complete with ruffles, lace, sequins, and ribbons. Her sneakers were changed into white leather shoes. A pearl necklace rested against her throat and long white gloves covered her hands and arms.

An Improbable Adventure at Grandma's House

70

Eight: Oakley's Temptation

Miraculously, she still held onto the giant lollipop.

For the second time, Oakley gasped in delighted astonishment. "It's so beautiful! *I'm* so beautiful," she exclaimed with spellbound eyes. She twirled around and the gown flared.

"If you come with me," invited the clown in a voice that seemed to drip with syrup, "I have a castle you can live in. You can wear your beautiful dress there."

"Is it far from here?"

"No, not far."

At that moment, Prince came charging out of the woods, barking and growling. He aimed straight for the clown. Before the clown could react, the dog bit him firmly on the leg. Right behind him came Luccan, waving a stick that looked much like a baseball bat. He saw the clown first and then Oakley.

"What are you doing here?" asked Luccan sternly. "Where are the others?"

The clown thrashed uselessly at Prince, who would not let go, yelling a string of bad words at both the dog and Luccan.

Oakley didn't know how to understand the commotion. "Stop!" she yelled at Prince. "You're hurting the clown."

"He's not really a clown, Oakley!" Luccan took her by the shoulders. "He's the Trickster I warned you about."

"But he was nice to me. He gave me my favourite candy and… and this beautiful dress."

"It's fake! All of it."

"No. It's delicious, and the dress is the most beautiful I've ever had," insisted Oakley. "He said I could wear it in his castle."

Luccan placed a finger under Oakley's chin and lifted it to look into her eyes for the second time that day. "Oakley, if you go with the Trickster… er, the clown… you will never see your Mommy and Daddy again. You will live in his castle like a prisoner."

Those words broke the spell. "I want to go home and see my Mommy," said Oakley, now worried.

She started to cry. Instantly the beautiful gown disappeared and she was back to wearing her own clothes and shoes. The lollipop turned out to be a dandelion, limp and slimy from being licked.

"No!" howled the Trickster. "You always foil my plans! You are a menace, Mr. Luccan. I hate you!"

For an instant, his many colours turned into shades of black, grey, and purple and he grew to a

Eight: Oakley's Temptation

monstrous size. Just as quickly, he returned to his much smaller shape.

"The Great One hates your lying, cheating ways, and so do I," yelled Luccan. "Shame on you for trying to trick an innocent little girl who's not even from Avery."

"My powers reach beyond Avery. It doesn't matter where in the Beyond she's from," hissed the Trickster. "Call off your ugly hound."

"Only if you leave my district. You aren't welcome here."

The Trickster sneered. "Oh piffle. You say that every time we cross paths. I can come and go wherever I like and you can't stop me."

"The Great One will have something to say about that," warned Luccan.

"Don't mention Him to me."

As soon as Prince let go, the Trickster vanished into thin air, surprising Oakley all over again.

"Where did he go?" she wondered.

"Someplace where he can lick his wounds, I suppose." Luccan sounded relieved. "Are the others at my cabin?"

Oakley hung her head in embarrassment. "No, Mr. Luccan. I came by myself."

"I hope you won't do that again. You understand that to be here alone in a strange land is dangerous, don't you?" said Luccan more gently.

"Yes, sir. I want to go home now. I'm feeling sick to my stomach and itchy all over," she said, scratching at her arms.

Luccan looked at her suspiciously. "Did the Trickster give you something to eat?"

Oakley nodded. "He gave me a giant lollipop. I had quite a lot of it."

"Ahhh. Then that's what's making you sick. You'll have to come with me so I can fix you up with some medicinal tea."

By the time they reached Luccan's cabin, Oakley felt so itchy that she couldn't sit still. Luccan hung a kettle over the fire, to which he had added some herbs and powders. A few minutes later, he handed her a mug of the steaming brew.

Oakley looked at the red liquid and expected it to taste bad. To her surprise and relief, though, it was delicious, kind of like peppermint and cinnamon and roses combined.

Eight: Oakley's Temptation

Luccan also gave her some crackers that tasted like dried honey.

After two mugs, the itching had stopped and Oakley felt lots better. She returned home soon afterward through the picture frame portal, this time a wiser little girl.

CHAPTER NINE
Strange Barking Sounds

Aidyn looked up from playing on her tablet, frowned, and looked over at Sydney, who was napping on his dog cushion. Chase glanced up from the superhero book he was reading.

"I just heard a dog bark," Aidyn said, puzzled. "But Sydney's asleep, so it can't be him."

"Me too," said Chase. "It must be a dog on the street outside."

Aidyn heard the barking again. "There! There it is."

"I heard it, too."

Both kids listened intently, and then Chase got up to see if there was a dog barking outside on the street. There wasn't.

"You know, I think we've heard these barks before." An idea was forming in Aidyn's head, but the thought was unbelievable.

Nine: Strange Barking Sounds

Chase agreed. "They sound like Mr. Luccan's dog, Prince."

"That's what I was thinking, but it's impossible! We're not even at Grandma's house. How could we be hearing Prince?"

"Well, if it is Prince," replied Chase, "he sounds like he's really upset, or really excited about something."

"You're right. I think we should try to get to Grandma's house and figure it out from there."

They went outside and found their dad in the garage.

"Dad, could you take us to Grandma's house for a short visit?" Aidyn pleaded.

"Sure, you can come along for a ride to Grandma's place," Dad said. "I was just about to take these bags of trash to be burnt on Papa's burn pile."

A few minutes later, they were on their way to Grandma's house.

"Woof! Woof!" barked Bodhi, bouncing all over his bed as if he had ants in his pants.

"Stop it!" scolded Kipton. "I'm trying to read and I can't concentrate with all the noise you're making."

An Improbable Adventure at Grandma's House

Nine: Strange Barking Sounds

"I can't help it. I hear a dog in my head. I'm trying to talk to it."

"Don't be ridiculous. If you're going to be noisy, do it somewhere else. Go bother Mommy for a while."

Just then, Oakley walked into the boys' bedroom. "Kipton, do you hear a dog barking? It's not Cedar, because I checked. He's in the backyard sprawled out on the deck chewing on a toy. But I hear a dog barking, and it sounds like he's right next to me."

"Then you're just as crazy as Bodhi," said Kipton sarcastically. "He thinks he has a dog in his head."

"But that's just what it sounds like!" declared Oakley. "A dog in my head is barking like he's mad, or maybe just really excited. He won't stop."

Bodhi started to bounce again. "See, I told you."

Kipton was going to say they'd gone bonkers, but then he froze.

"Now I hear it," he said, surprised and awed. "I'm sure it's impossible, but it sounds like Prince."

"I thought so, too," Oakley frowned. "But we're nowhere near the picture in Grandma's house. It doesn't make any sense."

"The picture in Grandma's house doesn't make sense either, yet we actually went into it. I wouldn't believe it if it hadn't happened to us," said Kipton. "If we were at Grandma's house, we could check the picture and see if it came alive again. We could find out if Prince was in trouble or something…"

"Do you kids want to go for a ride to Grandma and Grandpa's place?" called their dad from the foot of the stairs. "I have to return some tools to Papa's shop. You can come along if you want."

In one movement, all three kids scrambled down the stairs without even one second of hesitation.

When Aidyn and Chase pulled into their grandparents' driveway, they were surprised to see another of their cousins standing near the house. At thirteen, Finn was a few months older than Aidyn. He and his mom had come to the acreage on the invitation of Grandma to collect some fruits and vegetables ready for picking.

Nine: Strange Barking Sounds

The dust had barely settled from Aidyn and Chase's arrival when Kipton, Oakley, and Bodhi also showed up. They all ran to where Finn was standing near the garage and greeted each other enthusiastically. Nobody said anything about hearing a dog bark—that is, until Finn started looking around, as if he was seeking something or someone.

"What's the matter with you?" Aidyn asked. "What are you looking for?"

Finn seemed puzzled. "I hear Shep barking, but he doesn't seem to be anywhere around."

"Does the barking seem like it's coming from inside your head?" asked Chase.

"Yeah. I guess you could put it that way."

"Me too! Me too!" said Oakley and Bodhi at the same time.

"I hear a dog barking frantically," said Kipton. "It sounds like Mr. Luccan's dog."

"It must mean something," Aidyn said.

Meanwhile, Finn appeared thoroughly bewildered. "Like what?"

Aidyn took charge. "If you can hear a dog barking inside your head and you haven't been in Grandma's picture before, you need to come with us."

An Improbable Adventure at Grandma's House

She led the troop of cousins into Grandma's house and living room.

The picture was alive, just as the cousins had suspected it might be. Chase and Kipton went into the painting first, followed by Oakley.

"What the…!" sputtered Finn.

"We'll explain later," Aidyn assured him. "Just go into the picture like the other kids."

Finn followed the example of his younger cousins and climbed over the picture frame. Aidyn grabbed Bodhi, deposited him inside, and then clambered in after him.

"This is so weird." Finn pinched his arm. "Where are we? Am I dreaming or is this for real?"

"You're in the land of Avery," said Aidyn, but she couldn't say more yet because suddenly Prince charged out of the forest and greeted them with yelps, barks, and licks on their faces.

CHAPTER TEN
Luccan Is Rescued

The dog ran circles around the children, barking with joy.

"All right, all right, Prince. We get it!" laughed Aidyn, trying to slow down the dog with a hug.

Prince barked, whined, yelped, and made a short howl while running to the edge of the forest and then back again.

"He's trying to talk to us like he does to Mr. Luccan," observed Chase.

"Sorry, Prince," said Kipton. "None of us can speak dog."

Prince whined again and latched onto Oakley's wrist. He gently tried to pull her off the road.

"I think he wants us to follow him," said Oakley.

Prince barked as if to agree and then took her wrist again.

An Improbable Adventure at Grandma's House

"Lead on, buddy," said Aidyn.

They followed the path only a short distance. Before they could get to Luccan's cabin, though, Prince veered unexpectedly to the right.

The children stopped, unsure what to do. The dog barked sharply, urging them to keep coming.

Chase stepped off the beaten path. "I guess we're supposed to go this way."

"I sure hope you guys know what you're doing," said Finn doubtfully. "None of this is making any sense to me. And I don't want us to get lost on top of everything else."

"We're safe with Prince. I'm sure about that," replied Aidyn. "He's sort of a guard dog who helps Mr. Luccan with his forestry work. No need to worry."

Aidyn stopped to carry Bodhi on her back, as he was having trouble keeping up and getting fretful about it.

Prince led them through the woods in a zigzag pattern that made them feel like they were getting farther and farther away from Luccan's cabin.

Suddenly the dog stopped and whined over a gaping hole in the forest floor. The children stopped

Ten: Luccan Is Rescued

as well and peered over the edge. The hole was deep and dark.

"What is this?" Finn wanted to know. "A well? A mineshaft?"

A human spoke out of the depths. "Praise the Great One!" rang the voice of Luccan. "He's sent help at last!"

"It's Mr. Luccan!" cried Chase.

The dim light of the forest made it hard to see clearly in the dark, but they recognized the forester several feet down.

"How did you get down there? Are you hurt?" cried Aidyn.

"When did this happen?" Kipton asked.

"We'll save the stories for later," replied Luccan. "Right now I need you to get to my cabin and bring back rope and a hatchet."

Aidyn frowned. "We don't know where your cabin is from here."

"Prince will guide you," assured Luccan.

It was agreed that only Finn and Aidyn would fetch what was needed. The four younger kids were to stay and keep Luccan company until they returned.

An Improbable Adventure at Grandma's House

Ten: Luccan Is Rescued

Not long after Finn and Aidyn left, Chase became aware of a bad smell. It was different than skunk, but just as bad.

"Something stinks," he said, screwing up his nose.

"The Trickster is coming," hollered Luccan from the pit. "Hide. Now."

The four children scrambled to get behind a thick, prickly shrub. A moment later, something appeared—a cross between an old man and an ogre. It wore black clothing from head to toe.

Kneeling at the edge of the pit, the creature peered into the dark and cackled derisively.

"Still can't find your way out?" hissed the black figure. "Ha! And you never will. I finally have you where you can't interfere with me anymore. You're finished, and good riddance!"

"I trust the Great One," shouted Luccan. "He will decide if and when I'm finished."

"Five days and nights you have lain in my snare, and the Great One hasn't bothered to rescue you. You are a fool to trust Him with *anything*."

"The Great One can rescue me anytime He deems right. But even if He doesn't, I'll never join your cause, Trickster." As soon as Luccan finished speaking, he began to sing an anthem that praised the Great One.

The Trickster covered his ears with his hands. "Stop. Stop! Your noise hurts my ears," he crabbed.

In response, Luccan sang a little louder.

Since Finn and Aidyn were older and could run fast, they reached Luccan's cabin quickly. Prince scratched at the door until Aidyn opened it. Then he dashed inside, with Finn and Aidyn following behind.

The dog poked his nose under Luccan's bed and began to pull out a coil of rope.

"The rope! Good dog." Finn scanned the room for more rope and found another coil.

Aidyn rummaged through the kitchen.

"Now whatcha doing?" asked Finn. "We gotta get back with the rope and not waste any time."

"I'm looking for something in which to take him some water and a bit of food," explained Aidyn.

They found a tin of biscuits and an empty jar which she promptly filled with water.

Ten: Luccan Is Rescued

They began the return trip, but Finn stopped suddenly. "I forgot the hatchet," he said, annoyed with himself.

"Well, hurry!" scolded Aidyn. "We're taking too long."

When they were sure the Trickster was gone, the four kids crept out from behind the thorn bush.

"Are you okay?" asked Oakley, very concerned as she peered down the hole.

"I will be as soon as the others get back with the rope," said Luccan, trying to sound cheerful.

They heard a commotion coming towards them and soon Prince bounded into view with Finn and Aidyn following.

"I brought you some water and biscuits," said Aidyn, breathless.

"Good thinking. That was very thoughtful of you," said Luccan appreciatively as they slowly let down the water and biscuits by rope. "This is like a banquet after all the nuts and acorns the squirrels fed me!"

Finn took charge of the ropes. The nearest sturdy tree stood about two meters away from the deep hole. He took one of the ropes and tied it around the tree, making a secure knot. He then attached the second rope to the first with a square knot.

"Do you want me to send down the hatchet?" enquired Finn.

"Yes." Luccan had to be patient. "Tie it to the end of the rope."

After it was lowered, Luccan used the hatchet to notch some toeholds as high as he could reach. They would help him when he scaled the smooth walls of the pit.

Finally, he tied the rope around his waist so the hatchet hung by his knees.

"I'm ready to start coming up," Luccan announced.

The children watched with great suspense as Luccan slowly scaled the walls of the pit, going hand over fist on the rope and using the notches to steady his toes.

At one point he slipped and fell back a ways. Oakley let out a short shriek.

"It's all right," said Luccan, concentrating on his work. He began to climb again and soon had his

Ten: Luccan Is Rescued

head aboveground. A minute more and he fell onto the ground, home free.

The children clapped in relief. Prince licked Luccan's face and woofed for joy.

Questions poured out of the children's mouths with everyone talking at once, and Luccan had to hold up his hand, symbolically calling for quiet.

"Let's go home and tell our stories around a campfire," he said.

CHAPTER ELEVEN
Much Is Explained

After Luccan had Aidyn mix up a batch of biscuit dough, and after he bathed himself in the stream not far from his cabin, and after they had eaten a delicious supper of sausages and baked biscuits roasted over a campfire, they all sat in a circle on the grass to share their stories.

"I was doing the daily patrol of my district of the royal forest, watching out for the poachers who sometimes come to take game animals or cut trees illegally," began Luccan. "I noticed some trees were marked with red ribbons. Curious, I began to follow the trail of ribbon-marked trees. I wasn't watching the ground ahead of me closely when suddenly I took a step into the air and fell feetfirst into that hole. It wasn't deep enough to hurt me, but I was stunned. Prince barked furiously but couldn't help.

Eleven: Much Is Explained

The hole was easily twice as deep as I am tall and the walls were hewn smooth. No way could I get out by my own efforts. But when I recovered from my shock, I wondered about the hole I was in and how it had come to be there. I thought I knew every inch of this forest, including the location of any abandoned wells or mineshafts."

"That's the first thing that came to my mind," offered Finn, who listened closely.

"But there was no evidence of the pit having a former use. I began to think it was dug purposely to trap something… or someone. A little while later, my hunch proved right. The Trickster soon stood over the hole and rubbed his hands together with glee that he had trapped me so handily. I asked him why he had gone through so much trouble to snare me and he replied that he was angry that I had thwarted so many of his plans, especially lately when I rescued a little girl from his slippery trickeries."

Upon hearing this, Oakley blushed. She hoped he wouldn't tell the others that she was the little girl. He did not.

"Every day he came to check to make sure I was still captured," Luccan added. "And to mock me for being loyal to the Great One."

"What about food and water?" asked Kipton. "Weren't you starving?"

"My needs were looked after by my animal friends," replied Luccan. "Squirrels shared their nuts and acorns with me. Racoons brought me juicy apples and pears as a substitute for water. Birds dropped me some earthworms, too, but I didn't get hungry enough to try those. Prince wanted to help, of course. He can't use his legs like arms or his paws like fingers, though, so I sent him to check whether you kids had come through the portal. I didn't want you wandering around Avery while I was held up in the pit. With the Trickster on the loose, he's more dangerous than ever."

Oakley felt sorry for all the trouble Luccan had gone through. "Weren't you cold and lonely?"

"Not really. I called on the Great One, and He kept me company. Even though I missed the comforts of my cabin, His warm presence strengthened and encouraged my heart every day."

Eleven: Much Is Explained

"Why didn't the Great One get you out?" asked Chase solemnly.

"I asked Him to, even pleaded," answered Luccan. "His answer to me was that I must be patient for a while, that help would come at just the right time."

Chase felt confused by this. "But He could have done it Himself, couldn't He?"

"Yes. The Great One doesn't need anyone's help with anything," agreed Luccan. "Since I was stuck in the pit, I had time to do a lot of thinking. I believe the Great One wanted to share my adventure with others, which turned out to be you from the Beyond. He wants to participate in the life stories of His loyal subjects. They become more interesting when he weaves other people and situations into our predicaments. When the Trickster comes around to make mischief, or worse, the Great One turns it inside-out to make something good from it. That is, if we let Him."

Finn nodded. "We have a saying in our world about that. When life hands you lemons, make lemonade."

"That's exactly right," said Luccan. "While the Trickster thought I was wasting away as his prisoner,

Eleven: Much Is Explained

the Great One was my companion and teacher in the cold dark. Besides that, I improved on my animal language skills and learned a couple more. I can now add mouse and chipmunk to my linguistic abilities!"

"That's amazing," said Oakley with a smile. "I wish I could talk to animals in their own languages."

"Me too," added Bodhi.

"I even made up a song to help cheer myself up," added Luccan shyly.

Aidyn pleaded, "Sing it for us!"

The tune Luccan sang had all the qualities of a lullaby that comforted the soul. The words recalled the love and faithfulness of the Great One and the anticipation of someday living in His realm where everything is always well and good and there's no Trickster to spoil things. The beauty of the song made their hearts ache with yearning.

"Sing it again," said Bodhi once Luccan had finished.

Luccan shook his head. "I'd like to hear how all of you came to Avery at the same time to carry out a rescue mission. Especially when you don't even live in the same households."

An Improbable Adventure at Grandma's House

"We have a pet dog at home," began Aidyn. "But we heard barking clear as day, and it wasn't coming from him, nor were there any dogs outside. We figured out that we were hearing Prince in our heads. That's when we decided to get to Grandma's place and see if the picture was alive. If it really was Prince, we needed to find out why. Prince was barking like crazy! Like he was upset about something."

"That's exactly what happened to us," Kipton said. "Bodhi started it, and then Oakley and me heard it, too. The sound was so real that it seemed like the dog was in the same room with us. The odd thing is that just as we figured out it was Prince, our dad asked if we wanted to go with him to Grandma's farm. Of course we said yes!"

Chase smiled. "Us too. Our dad already had a reason to go anyway."

Luccan turned his attention to the newest visitor. "What about you, Finn?"

"I just came to the farm with my mom to pick veggies from the garden," said Finn. "I heard barking, too, but Grandma's dog was in the shop with Papa."

Luccan chuckled happily. "It seems clear to me that the Great One operates in your world as well."

Eleven: Much Is Explained

"We think so, too," piped up Aidyn. "He goes by different names there, like God and our heavenly Father."

"Heavenly Father…" Luccan stroked his beard. "I like that. I like it a lot. What about the Trickster? He hinted to me that he roams other worlds as well."

Finn lowered his head. "Yeah, we have different names for him, too."

"Such as…?"

They all spoke up at once.

"Satan."

"The Devil."

"Lucifer."

"Humphff." Luccan grunted and shook his head. "The exciting part is this: do you see how the Great One lined up all these details? From the first time you came through the portal, Chase, He has brought a variety of people from all over His creation to play their parts so that it tells an amazing story only He could have put together."

"I never thought of it like that, but I see what you mean," said Aidyn thoughtfully. "I remember you wondering about the purpose behind us coming here from the Beyond. Now we know that the Great One was going to involve us in a rescue mission."

Chase couldn't wipe the smile from his face. "It was exciting!"

"And fun, too," added Kipton.

CHAPTER TWELVE

Goodbyes and a Word About Other Worlds

The campfire was soon reduced to red coals and ashes. Twilight set in and Luccan yawned. This was another clue that it was time to go home.

There wasn't much talking as the children walked the familiar path from Luccan's cabin to the portal. As usual, Prince led the way while sniffing for danger. Luccan came last, like the caboose on a train, to make sure no danger would touch them.

When they arrived at the main road, they found it empty—no clowns or anything else that could disturb the natural quiet.

"Can I ask you something, Mr. Luccan?" asked Aidyn thoughtfully.

"Of course. What is it?"

An Improbable Adventure at Grandma's House

102

Twelve: Goodbyes and a Word About Other Worlds

"For me, this all started when the paintings in Grandma's house seemed to burst to life at the same time. The ocean pictures were leaking water. The autumn picture was super windy. I could even stick my hand through the mirror in the dining room. Are they all connected, do you think? Do they all lead to Avery? Why would the Great One do that?"

Luccan didn't answer immediately. "I don't really know, child, how these things work. Have those other pictures come alive again since that first time?"

"I don't think so. Not that I noticed anyway."

"It might be that the Great One was making sure He got your attention by bringing them all to life and then narrowing it down to just this one painting. Or maybe it's a clue that other adventures await you in the future. What you must do is pay attention, Aidyn." As Luccan spoke, he sounded like a schoolteacher, or maybe a parent. "And that goes for the rest of you children. Go about your days being aware of the Great One all the time. Talk to Him about everything and take time to be quiet so you can hear His voice, not unlike the way you heard Prince barking for your attention."

An Improbable Adventure at Grandma's House

Oakley suddenly looked very sad. "Are we ever going to see you again?"

"I don't know for certain, but I doubt it, sweetheart. I suspect you have fulfilled your purpose for coming here. Even if we never meet again, I'm sure I will never forget you."

"Me neither." Oakley reached up and hugged his neck.

One by one, each of the children embraced Luccan and murmured a sad goodbye—that is, all except Finn. He shook his hand instead, mumbling something about not being the hugging type.

They took turns climbing back through the portal so they wouldn't fall on top of each other on Grandma's sofa. Aidyn had to hold Finn's hand, since he didn't know how to distinguish the autostereogram image of the picture from Avery's side of it.

As soon as they were through, Finn looked back at the picture and discovered that it had once again turned into just a regular painting of a tall forest with a country road winding down the centre.

"Unbelievable!" pronounced Finn.

"No," declared Chase. "Believable!"

BIBLICAL THEMES

…what does the Lord your God require of you? He requires only that you fear the Lord your God, and live in a way that pleases him, and love him and serve him with all your heart and soul. (Deuteronomy 10:12)

[The Devil] was a murderer from the beginning. He has always hated the truth, because there is no truth in him. When he lies, it is consistent with his character; for he is a liar and the father of lies. (John 8:44)

Stay alert! Watch out for your great enemy, the devil. He prowls around like a roaring lion, looking for someone to devour. (1 Peter 5:8)

Resist the devil, and he will flee from you. Come close to God, and God will come close to you. (James 4:7–8)

God's way is perfect. All the Lord's promises prove true. He is a shield for all who look to him for protection. (Psalm 18: 30)

The Lord directs the steps of the godly. He delights in every detail of their lives. (Psalm 37:23)

[God] alone is my refuge, my place of safety; he is my God, and I trust him. For he will rescue you from every trap... (Psalm 91:2–3)

...whenever we have the opportunity, we should do good to everyone—especially to those in the family of faith. (Galatians 6:10)

Now all glory to God, who is able, through his mighty power at work within us, to accomplish infinitely more than we might ask or think. (Ephesians 3:20)

Walk with the wise and become wise; associate with fools and get in trouble. (Proverbs 13:20)

Wait patiently for the Lord. Be brave and courageous. Yes, wait patiently for the Lord. (Psalm 27:1)

ABOUT THE AUTHOR

Sandra Vivian Konechny is mother to two sons and two daughters, grandmother to nine grandchildren, and great-grandmother to two great-grandchildren. She and her husband Michael of forty-nine years live as retirees on an acreage northwest of Saskatoon, Saskatchewan.

Her passion for story and dialogue began as a youngster playing with paper dolls and giving the dolls scenarios to act out and lines to say. Apart from writing short stories, crafting. sewing, quilting, and counted cross-stitch (she has published several original patterns), she is kept occupied by baking, gardening, and doing crossword puzzles and word games. She also taught a Bible Study Fellowship class for nine years. She holds a bachelor of arts from the University of Manitoba with a major in English.

This is her first children's novel. In 2006, she published *When God Asks You...* with Word Alive Press, in which she examines and discusses thirteen questions in the Bible that God asked various individuals. She has also adult fiction under the series title *The Minitonas Diaries*, also published by Word Alive Press.

ABOUT THE ILLUSTRATOR

Clayton Markson lives in Osler, Saskatchewan with his wife, Whitney, of twenty-one years. They have four sons and two grandchildren.

While he loves to draw, a career in heavy-duty mechanics with accreditation as a Red Seal Endorsed Truck and Transport mechanic serves as his day-job.

He began drawing as a small boy and did it regularly until he broke his arm in grade ten. Then his fingers wouldn't work the same. Later, after he married and his sons came on the scene, he began to draw for them (and his nieces and nephews). The difficulty with his fingers had passed and his images became 'good' again. While he enjoys drawing almost anything, scary things are the most fun.

His desire is to use his talents and creativity for God's glory.